THE GHASTLY MCNASTYS

Lyn Gardner is theatre critic for the *Guardian* and goes to the theatre five or six times a week, which should leave no time for writing books . . . But actually she has written several children's books, including the very successful *Olivia* series. She lives by Richmond Park.

Ros Asquith is a cartoonist for the *Guardian*, and has written and illustrated many books. *Letters from an Alien Schoolboy* was shortlisted for the Roald Dahl Funny Prize, and *The Great Big Book of Families*, which she illustrated, won the SLA Information Book Award. She lives in North London.

THE GHASTLY McNASTYS

FRIGHT IN THE NIGHT

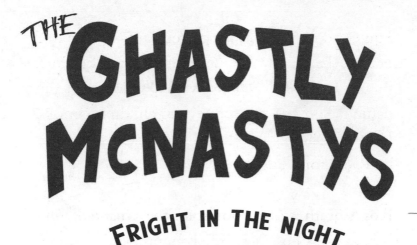

LYN GARDNER & ROS ASQUITH

Piccadilly

For Captain KJG – L.G.

To Lola, Lenny and Lucille – R.A.

First published in Great Britain in 2014
by Piccadilly Press
A Templar/Bonnier publishing company
Northburgh House, 10 Northburgh Street, London, EC1V 0AT
www.piccadillypress.co.uk

A catalogue record for this book is available
from the British Library

ISBN: 978–1–84812–392–2 (paperback)

1 3 5 7 9 10 8 6 4 2

Printed in the UK by Clays Ltd, St Ives plc
Cover illustration by Ros Asquith

WARNING!

Please keep this book shut
at all times, even when
you are reading it.

PARTICULARLY WHEN YOU
ARE READING IT.

If you dare to ignore this
advice do not be surprised if
the McNastys jump out from
the pages and give you fleas,
nits and nightmares.

The McNastys may try to
escape from the pages, and
if they do things could turn
VERY NASTY indeed.

These are the sorts of things that will come your way if you let the McNastys escape these pages.

~~Chapter 342~~

(Do not be utterly ridiculous. You cannot begin
a book with Chapter 342 as this would be
very confusing for everyone and like starting
the alphabet with N or eating fish and chips
and strawberry ice cream for breakfast.)

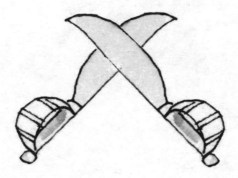

Chapter 1

Jamie Fried-Trout, the cabin boy, was standing high up in the crow's nest on the mast of the fishing trawler, *The Good Hope*. He had been chosen as lookout because he was the only member of the

3

crew who was fit enough to climb up to the crow's nest. But he was not an ideal choice because he suffered from terrible seasickness and was always too busy shouting, 'Oops, sorry!' to all those he was being sick over on the deck below to notice anything on the horizon.

The Good Hope

Since Jamie had been lookout, *The Good Hope* had sailed into the world's biggest iceberg (which immediately melted in shock, causing sea levels to rise dangerously), collided with Australia (which had shifted several hundred metres to the right), and hit Canada (which now had a terrible dent in it). Jamie had been obliged to say, 'Oops, sorry!' rather a lot recently.

Worst of all had been the giant squid, which had got completely tied up in knots in its own tentacles after *The Good Hope* ran into it.

Jamie had apologised profusely and promised that he would never eat calamari again (not even when it is grilled with garlic, lemon juice and olive oil, which is scrumptious). But the giant squid was in no mood for apologies and when it eventually untied itself, it waved its tentacles like a fist at Jamie and swam away with revenge so clearly glinting in its eye that Jamie began to wish that his parents had never met.

How he longed to be back on dry land, preferably in Little Snoring with his cousin Trevor Augustus Trout, otherwise known as Tat, and Tat's best friend, Hetty. Hetty was the cleverest girl in the world and would surely know how to cure seasickness and placate vengeful squid. She knew everything. Well, almost everything, as she did not know

that guinea pigs yawn to show anger or that
fleas can survive for over a year without
eating, or where Captain Syd's lost treasure
was buried in Little Snoring.

But she and Tat were working on finding
the treasure with the help of the treasure
map, which had been found in the ancient

Little Snoring Castle. Jamie was going to help them.

Jamie knew that it was essential for them to find the treasure as soon as possible because Tat had told him that, as usual, the Trout family fortunes were in a very unfortunate state. Every time Mrs Trout tried to make ends meet, the ends wriggled further apart like over-excitable worms. Mrs Trout had taken on an extra part-time job in the local tearooms, and Mr Trout was trying to invent things, hoping to add to his

meagre earnings as Little Snoring's lighthouse keeper. So far he had invented the wheel, electricity, ice cream and luminous paint and had been very disappointed to discover that somebody had invented all of them before him.

He was now working on a top-secret new invention. Tat had told Jamie he thought it had something to do with glue.

The ship had been due to arrive in Little Snoring a few days before, and was already late because of bad weather. Jamie was worried they might not get to Little Snoring in time for the annual Fancy Dress Junior Disco. Jamie already had his costume made and hidden under his bunk in his cabin. He was planning to go as the vengeful ghost of Captain Syd. He hoped to scare everyone witless.

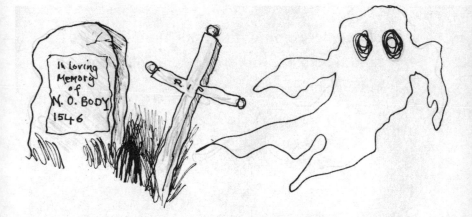

In loving
Memory
of
N. O. BODY
1546

R I P

But before they reached Little Snoring, he was hopeful that he might yet redeem himself with the crew of *The Good Hope*. So when he heard a strange noise coming from somewhere out at sea he tried to forget his queasy tummy and be as alert as possible.

He put the telescope to his eye and saw a shark zigzagging its way across the ocean towards the ship. The shark appeared to be in some distress, but the really odd thing was the noise coming from it. Jamie listened hard. There was no doubt, he could hear it quite clearly.

This was no ordinary shark — it was a talking shark. It was also hiccupping very loudly.

'Talking, hiccupping shark, ahoy!' shouted Jamie. The captain of the trawler was so surprised that Jamie had spotted anything at all that she put the brakes on rather too hard and the boat skidded so sharply to the left that everyone fell over except Jamie, who was clinging to the mast very tightly.

The whole crew counted to ten, because in the hold they had a small cargo of dynamite that they were transporting for use in the Greater Snoring quarry, which was run by the trawler skipper's brother. But there was no explosion and

DYNAMITE

Turn off engine.
No mobile phones.
No matches
or silly business.
Flammable.
Handle with care.
Don't say you
weren't warned.
This is not a toy.

everyone heaved a sigh of relief. Jamie clambered down the mast and joined the captain and the rest of the crew, who were rubbing their squashed noses and staring over the side of the boat at the shark. There, a strange sight met their eyes.

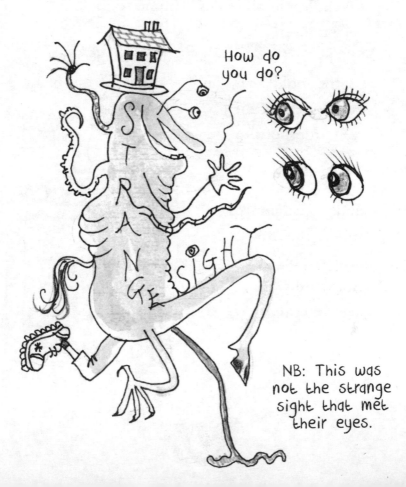

NB: This was not the strange sight that met their eyes.

Chapter 2

(2 is too too good, and twice as good as 1, which is often very naughty and has to be glued to the pages to make it stay there.)

Sharks are very hard to catch (not that *The Good Hope* ever tried, as it was a specialist fishing vessel and only ever caught fish fingers). But the shark they were looking at kept rising up out of the sea and putting

 its flippers
together as if it
was begging to be let aboard.
What's more, it was quite clearly talking.
Every time it opened its mouth the words
'Sweaty socks!' and 'Squeaky pants!' could
be heard. Its hiccups were getting worse too,
and its eyes more desperate.

'Bring out the nets,' shouted the captain.
It was not often that she felt sorry for a
shark, but this one was clearly in terrible
distress and needed help.

The sailors threw the net overboard, the
shark jumped into it, and everyone hauled it
up over the side of the boat and onto the
deck, where it fell with a bump.

'Ouch!' said two voices inside the shark.
The shark nodded desperately towards the
captain's knife, which was secured in her

HICCUP!

belt. Reluctantly,

the Captain took out her
knife, ready to cut down the middle of the
shark's belly. She looked into the shark's
eyes. The shark nodded again.

'Wait!' shouted Jamie. He remembered
that when he had terrible hiccups or a
stomach-ache he would sometimes feel
better if his mum rubbed his back very hard.
He ran over to the shark, motioned to the
other sailors to help him turn it on its front
and began to rub and pat the shark's back.
The shark's hiccupping grew louder, and
Jamie patted harder. Then all of a sudden
it gave an enormous

BUorrrP

(louder than a 10,000 ton meteor hitting the
Earth), opened its mouth very wide and two

strange, smelly, misshapen creatures slithered
out onto the deck.

'Sweaty socks,' groaned one.

'Squeaky pants,' moaned the other.

The pong coming from the creatures was
unbearable: like bad drains mixed with

maggoty fish and your big brother's smelly socks that have been left in a corner of the bedroom since the Easter before last.

'Poor shark!' said the captain. 'It must have accidentally swallowed these repulsive, repellent sea monsters.'

The two revolting creatures gave a shriek of anger and rose to their feet.

'I'm not repulsive! I am Captain Gruesome, and millions of people across the world consider me extraordinarily attractive, except I haven't met any of them yet,' said one, snatching the captain's knife and waving it threateningly.

'How dare you call me repellent! I'm Captain Grisly. I'm proud that so many admire me and I declare that I am as handsome as a wombat, as cunning as a crocodile and as ferocious as a Tasmanian devil.'

19

'And as smelly as a skunk,' remarked the trawler captain, which was brave, but rather foolish, as the McNastys advanced towards her so threateningly that even the sun took fright and hid behind a cloud.

'You won't be making any rude personal

And as smelly as a skunk.

CAPTAIN

remarks when you are walking the plank,' cackled Captain Gruesome, who was delighted to be released from the shark's belly and even happier that the opportunity to be ghastly and nasty had presented itself so soon.

He signalled to his brother, Grisly, who had found a suitable plank and secured it in place. The 423 fleas, two million nits, hundreds of mice and a ferret that had been living in Grisly's revolting bushy beard immediately rushed towards the plank. They just couldn't wait to get away from him. They sang as they marched and, if you listened hard, you could hear the tiniest of plops as each nit hit the sea.

'You next,' said Grisly to the shark, which shook its head at such stupidity and looked at him with utter contempt as it leapt overboard.

One by one, with Captain Gruesome using his knife to tickle their backs (which none of them found in the slightest bit funny) the trawler captain and crew were made to walk the plank. They went *SPLISH*, *SPLASH*, *SPLOSH* or *SPLAT* as they hit the water depending on whether they were fat or thin, tall or small.

'With any luck that nasty shark will be waiting to gobble them all up,' said Captain Gruesome, grinning happily at the thought.

Jamie was at the very back of the queue, which was moving far faster than he would have liked. He couldn't swim – although he could put his head underwater in the bath and hold his breath for a very long time. His father had always said that anybody who had seen how fat whales grew would know that swimming was a completely useless form of exercise, and had made him take up tiddlywinks instead (always playing with the window open so he got plenty of fresh air). Jamie was brilliant at tiddlywinks but tiddlywinks was not of the slightest use at this moment (my terrapin says he can't think of any life-threatening occasion when tiddlywinks would come in useful) and it was far too late to sign up for swimming lessons.

Like the others before him, Jamie was forced onto the plank at knifepoint, and he began to shuffle towards the end and oblivion. (Oblivion is the place name that is always found at the end of a plank hanging over a shark-infested sea and it has the postal code TH3 END. My terrapin was very keen that I should tell you this just in case you ever fancy sending a postcard to someone there, but do not expect to get a reply.)

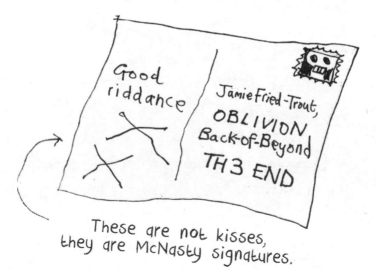

Good riddance

Jamie Fried-Trout,
OBLIVION
Back-of-Beyond
TH3 END

These are not kisses, they are McNasty signatures.

Jamie realised that with his next step he would walk into thin air and plunge to his doom (like oblivion but nastier, and smelling of cat-pee), when he felt himself being pulled back by the scruff of his neck.

'Hang on! We're going to need a cabin boy to boss about and be ghastly and nasty to on a regular basis, and you'll do, you revolting little pest,' said Captain Gruesome. 'Here, take this,' he said, reaching in his pocket and pulling out a pirate flag. 'Climb up the mast and raise the skull and crossbones.' He gave Jamie a kick on the behind and the boy began to climb upwards holding the flag.

'Sweaty socks,' cried Captain Gruesome happily as he found some tins of paint and leaned over the side of the boat and began to paint over the name *The Good Hope* and replace it with *The Rotten Apple II*. 'We're in command of our own ship again at last!

'And where are we going to sail her?' asked Captain Grisly.

'Don't be a ninny, Grisly. There is only one place on earth we want to be: Little Snoring. That's where Captain Syd's lost treasure is, just waiting for us to find it. Soon it will be all ours.'

'Provided those horrible children Tat and Hetty, that hideous cat called Dog, and that treacherous parrot called Polly haven't found it and snaffled it all first,' said Captain Grisly.

'Sweaty socks, we must hurry! Full speed ahead.'

Both brothers rushed to take control of the wheel and neither would give way so they began to biff and boff each other. Captain Grisly had taken off the ship's handbrake, and Captain Gruesome had turned on the engine. The ship began to spin round and round in circles.

Up in the crow's nest Jamie hung on for dear life. In the distance he could just see the shark swimming along with the entire crew clinging to her tail. It was heading for a small island.

The spinning was beginning to make him feel very queasy. He leaned out of the crow's nest and vomited with perfect accuracy all over the Ghastly McNastys below. 'Oops, sorry!' he cried.

The McNastys shook their fists and shouted at him to put up the pirate flag and then come down immediately. Jamie shook his head. He was too loyal to dream of flying any pirate flag on *The Good Hope*, and he definitely wasn't going to take orders from the McNastys. Jamie stuffed the pirate flag in his pocket and decided it was safest to stay where he was, up the crow's nest, out of reach of the pirates.

Chapter 3

(crowded with excitement.)

The Ghastly McNastys gazed upwards and were rewarded by a low-flying seagull plopping all over their noses.

The pirates shook their fists at Jamie Fried-Trout and shouted for him to come down yet again. Yet again, Jamie ignored them and took another swig from the large water bottle that he kept in the crow's nest. Then he took a bite from one of the jam sandwiches that, like his cousin, he always kept in his pocket for emergencies such as being kidnapped by pirates.

Jamie was only a few metres away at the top of the mast, but as far as the McNastys were concerned he could be on the moon or in Bigbottoms-by-the-Sea. He had ignored all the McNastys' attempts to lure him down for three whole days. The McNastys

wished they had made Jamie walk the plank with the others — by now he would have been fish food. They had tried shooting him with their catapults, but they had terrible aim and instead they had hit the moon with the dried snot balls they were using as ammunition and given the man in the moon a terrible headache. They had tried enticing Jamie down by smiling nicely (which was slightly more terrifying than being charged by rioting armoured armadillos) and telling him they were going to give him lemonade and chocolate cake (which they weren't, because they had already guzzled all the lemonade and eaten all the chocolate cake

The McNastys use snotballs in their catapults.

that they had found in the hold alongside several sticks of dynamite).

Now they had arrived in a secluded cove near Little Snoring, so getting Jamie down was a matter of urgency.

'Sweaty socks,' said Captain Gruesome, 'that boy is as stubborn as a mule and twice as ugly. Though not quite as furry.'

'Squeaky pants,' said Captain Grisly. 'We will have to starve him out.'

'We don't have time. He's got his own water and sandwiches. It could be weeks before he falls off his perch from lack of food and drink, and by then those revolting children and that nasty cat called Dog and that treacherous parrot will have found the treasure. Have another look in the book in case there is a suggestion that we've missed.'

Captain Grisly turned the pages of a

well-thumbed copy of *101 Ways to Dispose of Horrible, Horrendous and Hideous Children*, which they had borrowed from the Captain Bluebeard Memorial Library and had never taken back. They now owed £433 and 26p in fines and they had no intention of paying any of it.

The book offered excellent advice on boiling children in vats of oil, poisoning them with Truly Scrumptious, Perfectly Poisonous, Jam Sandwich-Flavoured Fudge, throwing them into pits full of angry vipers or putting them through a mincer and transforming them into frosted sugar icing  for cupcakes. Grisly thought the iced cupcakes sounded very tasty. But while the recipe began with *1. Catch your child* ... it gave no advice at all about how to go about it.

HOW TO TURN ANY CHILD INTO A USEFUL OR EDIBLE OBJECT

1. Catch your child.
2. Poison it.
3. Transform it.

[child] + [POISON]

+ [────── magic wand]

=

P.T.O.

If the fine hadn't been so much Captain Grisly would have taken the book back to the library and complained very loudly about the uselessness of the books they lent, and blocked out the words 'and', 'the', 'hippopotamus' and 'happy' in all the other library books in revenge.

The McNastys were beginning to feel quite sorry for themselves. They had escaped from the belly of the shark and hijacked *The Good Hope*. They had sailed the boat around the island of Little Snoring, far enough away not to be spotted, and they had put down anchor in an isolated natural cove on the uninhabited side of the island.

It had all passed without incident if you ignored the fact that every time they came on deck Jamie was sick all over them (the McNastys began to suspect he was using them as target practice). Oh, and there was their unfortunate run-in with a giant squid when they recklessly steered the boat into it, even though Jamie had shouted, 'Look out! Giant squid!' very loudly several times. Jamie apologised profusely to the squid, but the McNastys just laughed very rudely. As the squid untangled itself and swam away they shouted after it, 'Boo hoo. Armed but not very dangerous.'

They regretted it because the squid turned back and sprayed both of them in thick black ink. Jamie had clapped and cheered, and both the McNastys had had to take baths, which they hated as they had to look at themselves in the bathroom mirror, which always gave them a terrible fright. Having seen the McNastys' encounter with the squid, Jamie felt quite confident that he was no longer top of the giant squid's Most Wanted list.

WANTED

FOR CRIMES AGAINST SQUID

KATIE KIPPER
for discriminating against
those with multiple limbs.

BARRY BLOATER
for squid-battering and
deep frying.

JAMIE FRIED-TROUT
for vomit pollution.

**GRUESOME & GRISLY
MCNASTY**
for all of the above,
plus nose-picking, belching,
stealing toys, stamping on toddlers, etc, etc.
(Full list runs to six thousand and four pages.)

Now the McNastys knew (and unlike Hetty they seldom knew anything) that all they had to do was find out where Tat and Hetty were digging for treasure, wait until the children found it and then steal it for themselves.

But their dastardly plan was going wrong. If they left Jamie up the mast, what was to stop him swimming ashore as soon as they went and raising the alarm? They had to get him down and deal with him.

The McNastys could wait no longer. Even now they feared that diamonds were being uncovered and gold doubloons being counted by Hetty and Tat and taken to the Little Snoring Bank for safe-keeping. They had to get to Little Snoring as quickly as possible.

Captain Gruesome picked up an axe and swung the head hard against the mast. Captain Grisly picked up another axe and took aim too.

'Sweaty socks! This is hard work,' said Gruesome, whose idea of hard work was lying in a sun lounger eating ice-cream sundaes.

'Squeaky pants! This is exhausting,' said

Grisly, who was as lazy as a three-toed sloth and sometimes found putting on his socks in the morning so exhausting that he gave up bothering and just went back to bed.

It took ages but eventually they managed to cut their way through the wooden mast.

'Timber!' shouted Gruesome as the mast toppled down, narrowly avoiding crushing the McNastys as flat as (please choose your own answer):

A) Pancakes

B) Holland

C) An elephant after it has been run over by a steam roller.

The mast fell so its top end, where Jamie was holding on for dear life, was over the edge of the boat. For a moment Jamie clung onto it, his feet dangling over the sea below. But his fingers began to slip. The McNastys both raised their right hands and waved at him like a couple of kind uncles saying goodbye to a beloved nephew. They could see from Jamie's stricken face that he was losing the battle to hang onto the mast and they were thrilled.

'I can't swim!' he cried, hoping desperately that the McNastys would show mercy.

'Not our problem,' said the McNastys, annoyed they had gone to so much bother unnecessarily to cut down the mast. If they had known he couldn't swim they could just

No elephants were hurt in the making of this page.

have scuppered the spare rowing boat and left him stranded on the ship.

'Bye-bye, dear boy,' said Captain Gruesome sweetly.

'Adieu,' said Captain Grisly, who always felt that speaking in French lent an elegance to every occasion, including those that involved the permanent disposal of small irritating boys. Jamie knew that he could hold on no longer.

His fingers uncurled, his body dropped like a stone, and he plunged into the sea and disappeared under the water. The McNastys ran and peered over the side. They waited and then they waited some more. There was no sign of Jamie. They high-fived each other.

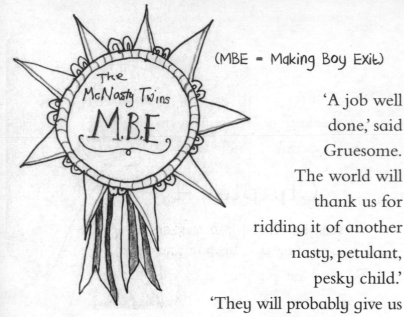

(MBE = Making Boy Exit)

'A job well done,' said Gruesome. The world will thank us for ridding it of another nasty, petulant, pesky child.'

'They will probably give us a prize. Maybe even a medal – a very big solid-gold one encrusted with diamonds,' said Grisly. 'Let's lower one of the rowing boats and head straight to Little Snoring.'

And they did, but only after they had gone into the hold and removed some sticks of dynamite in case the children had already found the treasure and taken it to the bank and they needed to blast their way into the vaults.

Chapter 4

(Can be divided into quarters
and read one bit at a time if you prefer)

Tat and Hetty were hot and tired. They had spent the morning digging for treasure by the cliffs. It was very close to the old abandoned graveyard, and at the point where the sparkling silvery sands of the

Little Snoring beach met the

BIG, SCARY, VERY DARK, DENSE FOREST

WHERE NO ONE IN THEIR RIGHT MIND
WOULD WANT TO GO

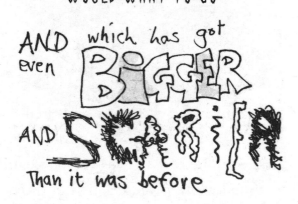

AND which has got even **BIGGER**
AND **SCARIER**
Than it was before

Few people did go there, so Tat and Hetty had been entirely undisturbed.

But Tat's heart wasn't in it. It was hard to get excited about treasure when he was so worried about the disappearance of *The Good Hope* and his cousin, Jamie.

Dog, who although he was a cat behaved like a dog, had spent the morning

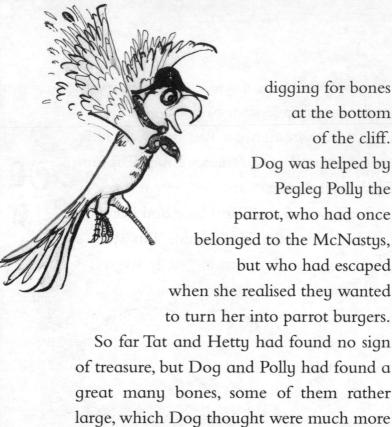

digging for bones
at the bottom
of the cliff.
Dog was helped by
Pegleg Polly the
parrot, who had once
belonged to the McNastys,
but who had escaped
when she realised they wanted
to turn her into parrot burgers.
So far Tat and Hetty had found no sign
of treasure, but Dog and Polly had found a
great many bones, some of them rather
large, which Dog thought were much more
valuable than diamonds or gold coins. Dog
didn't see the point of gold coins or
diamonds, as trying to chew either of them
would do your teeth no good at all.

Tat and Hetty were not disheartened

about their lack of success so far: after studying the map they'd found in the castle, they were certain that they were closer than they'd ever been to discovering Captain Syd's lost treasure.

Seeing her friend's sad face and hoping to cheer him up, Hetty said, 'I'm sure tomorrow will be the day, but we won't tell anyone, except our families. We don't want anyone else finding the treasure before us. And who knows, maybe *The Good Hope* will be found and Jamie will be here to share our good fortune.'

They didn't mind packing up early because it was the night of the Little Snoring Fancy Dress Junior Disco. Hetty and Tat were both going as skeletons and they needed to check their costumes. They had made them using some of the glow-in-the-dark paint that Tat's dad, Mr Trout, had invented before he realised that somebody had already invented it. There were pots of it in the garden shed. Tat would only give up hope for his cousin if Jamie failed to turn up tonight. Not even hungry mutant zombie armadillos would keep Jamie from the annual Fancy Dress Junior Disco.

On their way home, Hetty and Tat stopped off at the village shop to buy the fish fingers that Tat's dad, Mr Trout, had asked them to get for tea.

Dog and Pegleg Polly waited patiently outside. Dog had fallen asleep and was dreaming of gnawing a leg bone from a diplodocus. Dog was a cat who frequently bit off more than he could chew, and a 150 million-year-old diplodocus bone would be

quite something to chew on. Pegleg Polly was being fed birdseed by Mrs Slime, the McNastys' former second mate (regretful and reformed) who had just been to the shop

Mrs Slime,
the McNastys' ex-second mate

to buy 42 packets of tissues because she sneezed a great deal.

'No fish fingers, I'm afraid,' said Mrs Groan, the village gossip, who ran the Little Snoring village shop, an emporium of obscure cut-price bargains that nobody in their right mind would want to buy but often resorted to in an emergency. 'There has been a run on them since Monday when *The Good Hope* failed to dock in the Little Snoring Harbour as expected. People realised there might be a supply shortage. I could rummage around in the freezer and see if I've got any fish toes or elbows left, they've never been as popular as the fingers. Or I do have pickled herring and pink blancmange tartlets on special offer (such a clever, time-saving idea to put a main course and pudding together in a single flaky pastry case). Or I might be able to find the last jar of alligator and yaks' milk pâté; it has proved unexpectedly popular despite the fact it tends to bite the tongues of anyone who tries to eat it.'

Hetty shuddered. Mrs Groan shook her head sadly.

SPECIAL OFFERS

Wild roast Python souffle

Minced Armadillo with custard

Pan fried pineapple with cabbage sauce

'It's a terrible thing about *The Good Hope*. Your cousin Jamie was on board, wasn't he, Tat?'

Tat nodded sadly.

There had been much speculation in the *Little Snoring Gazette* (never the most reliable of newspapers) as to what had happened to the fishing vessel, which had so mysteriously disappeared. On Tuesday the headlines proclaimed that it had sunk in a storm; on Wednesday that it had been attacked by a giant squid; and this morning the newspaper speculated that the boat had been blown to smithereens by the small cargo of dynamite it was ferrying to the Greater Snoring quarry as a favour to the trawler skipper's brother.

Tat didn't know what to think, but he wasn't going to give up hope until after the Fancy Dress Junior Disco that he and Jamie had gone to together every year for the last five years. He knew that if Jamie didn't turn up tonight there was no hope. Jamie would never miss the Little Snoring Fancy Dress Junior Disco. He had won first prize for his costume for the last three years.

A man rushed into the shop. He was wearing a deerstalker and held a very large

magnifying glass in one hand and a pair of
handcuffs in the other, and he peered very
hard at Tat and Hetty through the
magnifying glass as if studying them for
clues. Tat found himself feeling guilty, even
though he hadn't done anything.

'Ah, Inspector Gullible Haddock, always on the job and looking for clues,' simpered Mrs Groan. 'The Inspector,' she told the children, 'is in charge of the investigation into *The Good Hope*. He is completely tireless.'

'I have left no stone unturned,' said Inspector Haddock, who indeed only that morning had looked under more than 200 stones and had found no trace of *The Good Hope* but had found a great many woodlice,

worms and a stag beetle, which had gripped his nose very hard with its pincers. He had come to the shop to buy a plaster.

'How are your investigations going?'

'I'm rooting out guilt everywhere I go, Mrs Groan,' said the Inspector, looking even harder at Tat and Hetty. 'Already today I have arrested nine boy scouts for helping old ladies across Little Snoring High Street without waiting for the green man at the traffic lights, and a woodchuck that kept chucking wood despite a very large sign forbidding it. Yesterday was an excellent day too: I arrested three children for reading under the bedclothes with a torch after their parents told them to go to sleep, and thwarted some men who claimed to be mending a hole in the road but who I, with my advanced powers of deduction, realised were semi-hardened criminals attempting to steal a cement mixer whose contents had spilled all over them.'

'But what about your investigation into the disappearance of *The Good Hope*?' asked Tat. 'Surely that's what you should be concentrating on?'

'Well, I don't want to boast,' said Inspector, who enjoyed nothing more, 'but I'm very good at juggling.'

'Oh,' said Mrs Groan, 'I had no idea that they taught circus skills in the police force.'

Inspector Haddock glared at her, but wondered whether circus might be a useful skill to add to his armoury of many talents that already included getting the wrong end of the stick and barking up the wrong tree. (This does not mean that Inspector Haddock thought he was a dog, just that he was not very good at solving crimes.)

'My brain is so advanced that I can do several things at the same time. That's why the world's criminals quake with fear whenever they hear my name. I have not only been cracking down hard on the shocking lawlessness in Little Snoring but I've made a major breakthrough in the case of *The Good Hope*. I have discovered that *The Good Hope* was a victim of Captain Syd's ghostly curse. I believe that the vessel was abandoned by its crew and sank after the ghost of Captain Syd appeared on board the ship.'

Inspector Haddock continued, 'It is well known that Captain Syd's ghost is prone to make appearances when anyone gets close to discovering his lost treasure buried in Little Snoring. As *The Good Hope* was heading for Little Snoring harbour, it could be that the ghost thought that the crew were looking for treasure. I have evidence: earlier in the week as I was walking home, I saw a strange glow and moving lights near the

BIG, SCARY, VERY **DARK**, DENSE FOREST

WHERE NO ONE IN THEIR RIGHT MIND WOULD WANT TO GO

AND which has got even BIGGER AND SCARIER than it was before.

I am quite certain it was the ghost of Captain Syd.'

'Actually —' said Hetty, who was about to tell Inspector Haddock that what he had seen was unlikely to be a ghost and more likely to be her and Tat digging for treasure after dark. But Inspector Haddock raised a hand to stop her.

'Do not interrupt me, little girl. My investigation is almost complete. I shall be making an arrest very soon. As long as my force stops bothering me with stupid unrelated incidents such as the appearance of a shark in Little Snoring Harbour surrounded by a cloud of fleas and nits and with a ferret sitting on its back.'

He shook his head and said wearily, 'They are such buffoons. It is hard for me to put up with their stupidity. But I assure you, an arrest is imminent. As far as I'm concerned the case is solved and closed. I'm now concentrating all my energies on investigating the mysterious disappearance of two pairs of outsize bloomers and a quantity of ladies' clothing from a washing line in Little Snoring this morning. I have a brain the size of a melon so I should have solved the mystery before the day is out.'

Hetty, who was very clever, maybe the cleverest girl in the entire world, knew that nobody's brain could be the size of a melon because it would not fit inside your head, and if it did it would make your head so heavy it wouldn't stay upright on your neck. She suppressed a loud snort. Tat glanced at his friend. She was clearly taking every word that Inspector Haddock was saying with a pinch of salt. (This does not mean that Hetty had eaten 487 pinches of salt – which is the exact number of words that Inspector Haddock has said so far, and please count if you don't believe me – as that would make her very thirsty and kill her. Taking something with a pinch of salt is not like taking sugar with your tea, it means that you disbelieve everything that someone is saying.)

Tat wasn't so sure. Maybe there was something in Inspector Haddock's theory. After all, it was the policeman's job to investigate things.

Hetty turned to the policeman and asked sweetly, 'Do tell me, Inspector, I'm very interested. How do you propose to go about arresting a ghost?'

Inspector Haddock frowned and then he said, 'I cannot share my plans with you, little girl, but I assure you that I will outwit the spook. I have my handcuffs at the ready.'

'I can't wait to see you make your arrest, Inspector,' said Hetty politely and then she turned to Tat. 'We must go. Your dad will be waiting for us.'

'Sorry about the lack of fish fingers. I could do you a two-for-one offer on shepherds if your dad wants to make a shepherds' pie,' said Mrs Groan, who was always eager to make a sale.

'No thank you,' said Tat firmly. He didn't think it was kind to go round eating shepherds or very fair on sheep, which would all get lost and baa very miserably

and keep everyone awake at night.

'Or I've got a cut-price toad only three weeks past its best-before date which comes with a free hole if you like toad in the hole,' Mrs Groan called after them. 'Or I've got fishcakes but only with strawberry and liquorice flavour buttercream icing . . .'

The children left the shop. Tat was very gloomy.

'I couldn't bear it if Jamie and the rest of the crew of *The Good Hope* were frightened to death by the ghost of Captain Syd.'

'Oh Tat,' said Hetty. 'Surely you don't believe in ghosts, do you?'

'Well,' mumbled Tat, 'I always think it's a good idea to keep an open mind about most things. What if Inspector Haddock's theory is right and the ghost of Captain Syd realises we are close to finding his treasure

Fish use their fingers
to cover their eyes
when they see
the McNastys.

and decides to come and get us next?'

'Come on, Tat, that policeman is completely clueless. If he thinks he can arrest a ghost, Inspector Gullible Haddock is even more stupid than his name suggests,' she said. 'I reckon that our Inspector wouldn't spot a clue even if it was waving at him from right at the end of his nose.'

Drat, this plaster is ticklish.

'What do you mean, Hetty?'

'Well, I've been thinking about that shark that the Inspector mentioned, turning up in Little Snoring harbour in a cloud of fleas and nits and with some mice and a ferret sitting on its back. I've never heard of something like that happening before. I just wonder whether there might be a connection between the appearance of the shark and the disappearance of *The Good Hope* and all her crew, because both are very unusual occurrences.'

Tat frowned. 'Maybe it's just a coincidence. Like lightning striking twice in the same place or Melancholy Smith in Year Four having a seagull plop on her head on the way to school every single morning for a week.'

'Maybe you are right,'

said Hetty. 'But when I think of fleas, nits, mice and rats, I also always think about the Ghastly McNastys, the nastiest (and smelliest) pirates ever to have sailed the Seven Seas. And when did we last see them? As they were swallowed by a shark.'

Tat gasped. 'Oh Hetty, do you think the McNastys may have something to do with the disappearance of *The Good Hope*?'

'Yes!' said Hetty. 'I'm also interested in those missing bloomers and women's clothes. I can't imagine how they are connected to the disappearance of *The Good Hope* but it's another very unusual occurrence. I don't think Little Snoring has ever had a washing-line thief before. Unlike Inspector Haddock we should keep all options and our eyes and ears open, and maybe we should do a bit of investigating of our own and try to find out if the Ghastly McNastys are responsible for the disappearance of *The Good Hope*.'

Chapter 5

Tat and Hetty, Tat's mum and dad and his little sister, Tallulah, scraped the last bit of food from their plates. Then they all removed their earplugs. Bubble and squeak, which is what Mr Trout had decided to cook for tea in the absence of any fish fingers, is delicious but all that squeaking from your plate can be quite off-putting, which is why it is a dish always best enjoyed while wearing earplugs. (Next time you are having bubble and squeak do be sure to mention the earplugs to your parents, who I can assure you will be delighted by the sheer brilliance of your idea.)

Sometimes the Trout family followed their
bubble and squeak with LOUD pudding —
so everyone had to put their earplugs back in.

'That was scrumptious,' said Mrs Trout, looking anxiously at the kitchen clock. (She was not looking anxiously at the kitchen clock because she was worried it was sickening for measles, but because Mrs Trout had taken a job in the Little Snoring Tea Rooms, and she didn't want to be late for her afternoon shift because it would be a busy one. On Wednesday afternoons Mrs Groan's shop was closed and anyone who wanted to hear the latest village gossip had to go to the tea rooms, which meant it was always full.)

'You've got plenty of time, my dear,' said Mr Trout, 'and we've got Baked Alaska for pudding.' (This did not mean that the Trout family were planning to eat the forty-ninth state of the USA, which would be much too big for a small family like the Trouts to

manage all on their own, and besides would never fit into their oven. Baked Alaska is a pudding made of cake piled high with ice cream, which is then smothered in meringue and baked in the oven at a high temperature for a short period of time. My terrapin says this is not cookery, but magic. I am inclined to agree.) 'Have you got room?'

Mrs Trout nodded. There is nobody in the world who hasn't got room for baked Alaska, not even a mum in a hurry.

'Mrs Trout,' said Hetty, 'would you mind if Tat and I accompanied you to the tea rooms for a short time?'

'Of course not, Hetty dear,' said Mrs Trout. 'But I thought you and Tat were going to make your costumes this afternoon.'

'We are,' said Hetty, 'but if I'm right and

the McNastys are behind the disappearance of *The Good Hope* and are making their way to Little Snoring, they'll be wanting to know exactly where Tat and I are digging for the treasure and how close we are to finding it. The tea rooms are the ideal place to spread a rumour around the village that the treasure is about to be found,

This is a random picture of Inspector Haddock gluing his nose to an elephant.

particularly as Mrs Groan always meets with her friends there on Wednesday afternoons. If the McNastys are hiding somewhere around, and they hear that, it will make them take action.'

'I'm a bit worried,' said Mr Trout with a frown. 'It's an invitation for every criminal in Little Snoring to go down to the site of your dig and try to steal the treasure.'

'Hetty and I thought about that,' said Tat. 'But as there are so few criminals in Little Snoring – except the ones that Inspector Haddock imagines – we thought we'd be pretty safe. And anyway, Inspector Haddock told Mrs Groan that he knows for certain that the ghost of Captain Syd is responsible for the disappearance of *The Good Hope*, so that news will be all around the village by now. Mrs Groan is such a gossip. People will be too frightened to go near the treasure site at night in case the ghost of Captain Syd really is on the loose and looking to take his revenge on anyone who tries to touch his treasure. The treasure site should be quite safe tonight, unless of course Inspector Haddock makes an arrest.'

'Which we all know will never happen. You can't arrest a ghost,' added Hetty. 'That Inspector Haddock has fewer brains than a pickled herring. He's blind to the fact that the flea-infested shark, the ferret, mice, nits, and the missing bloomers all suggest that Little Snoring's two most wanted criminals – the Ghastly McNastys – are on the loose.'

'But if you are right, Hetty, and the McNastys have escaped from the shark's belly, hijacked *The Good Hope* and made their way to Little Snoring to grab Captain

Syd's treasure, won't they stay away from the treasure site tonight too if they think there's a ghost about?' asked Tallulah. 'We know that they are such a pair of scaredy cats. They have proved that they are afraid of dentists and spiders, so don't you think it likely that they will be really scared of ghosts too?'

'Good question, Lulu,' said Hetty. 'But if the McNastys were responsible for the disappearance of *The Good Hope* they'll know that Inspector Haddock's theory about the ship being surprised by the ghost of Captain Syd is complete fishcakes. They'll see it as an opportunity to find and get their hands on the treasure without any interference. Anyway, the McNastys love treasure so much, nothing will put them off. Tat and I are banking on the fact that the lure of treasure will be too much for them to resist.'

'Yes,' said Tat, 'and when they turn up, Hetty and I will be waiting for them, and we'll find a way to make them tell us what happened to *The Good Hope*, and with any luck they will lead us to her and her crew.'

Mrs Trout shook her head. 'It all sounds very dangerous to me. The McNastys are

the nastiest and ghastliest pirates ever to have sailed the Seven Seas.'

'Don't worry, my dear,' said Mr Trout, patting his wife's arm. 'Have faith in Tat and Hetty. They've already outwitted the Ghasty McNastys twice before.'

'Yes, but what if it's third time lucky for those horrible pirates?'

'We've got plenty of help,' said Tat. 'We've got Dog and Polly on our side.' Dog wagged his tail enthusiastically, and Polly flew around the room squawking. 'And Mrs Slime is going to be on standby too in case of emergencies. You remember she used to be the McNastys' second mate? She hates the McNastys as much as we do. She still blames them for giving her an everlasting cold. Please, Mum, let us try. We know we can outwit the McNastys and maybe this time they'll stay away from Little Snoring for ever.'

Mrs Trout smiled and nodded. She knew how clever and brave Hetty and Tat were.

'And,' said Mr Trout, 'I've got just the thing that might come in handy. A tube of my latest invention: Trout's Miracle Glue.'

Mrs Trout looked doubtful.

'I do hope, my dear, that your miracle glue actually works, unlike Trout's Miracle Everlasting Ice, which melted in two seconds flat and Trout's Miracle Everlasting

Popping Corn that popped so miraculously that it spilled over the top of the saucepan and filled the entire downstairs of the house so we couldn't get in through the front door for two days.'

Mr Trout looked a little hurt at his wife's criticism.

'What's so miraculous about the glue?' asked Hetty.

'It's a glue and unglue in one handy tube. Apply it and it will stick anything to anything. Once it's dried completely you simply need to apply another dab and the things you've stuck together will miraculously unstick. Very useful if you've accidentally stuck the wrong things together, like that time your poor mother mistook superglue for lip salve and stuck her lips together.'

Mrs Trout shuddered at the memory.

'Does it actually work, Dad?' asked Tat.

'Ahem. Getting there,' said Mr Trout, a little sheepishly. 'It definitely sticks things together superbly. But I haven't quite got the unsticking bit right yet. There's some vital ingredient missing. I'm just trying to work out what it is. At the moment, once stuck it can only be unstuck after 24 hours using the specialist – and very expensive – methods currently employed in such situations, which would be unfortunate if you had accidentally superglued your bottom to the toilet seat. But when I've discovered the secret ingredient I think there will be a massive demand.'

Can you spot some glue disasters on these pages? (No prizes.)

I can dribble, but can't shoot!

'Of course there will be,' said Tallulah, rolling her eyes, 'because people are always going round supergluing their bottoms to toilet seats.'

'It happens more than you might think,' said Mr Trout. 'But for the moment, you need to take care with the glue. Or you could find yourselves in a very sticky situation.'

'We'll be careful,' said Tat.

'We are used to sticky situations,' said Hetty. And then she said thoughtfully, 'Thanks for the glue, Mr Trout, I think it could come in very useful.'

Reward Offered

There were a great many excellent words on these two pages (in fact some of the best ones I have ever written). Unfortunately the glue used to stick them down was not Trout's Miracle Glue but a glue of very inferior quality and they have fallen off and rolled away on the floor. Some have been spotted being carried away by a family of hungry mutant zombie armadillos.

WORD

The police have advised that on no
account should they be approached as
they are armoured and dangerous.
But if by any chance you find any of
the words lying about, please return
them to this page immediately.
They will be easy to identify as
belonging to me as they all begin
and end with a letter of the alphabet.

ADJECTIVE

THE
PINK
Aphid
AMAZING
WOOF
MRS·SLIME
JELLY
FROG
SNOWBALL
Octopus
KISS
TURNIP
ARM
TOE
McNASTY
pimple
cloud

Chapter 6

The Little Snoring tea rooms were unusually full. Word had spread very quickly around the village from Mrs Groan's shop that Chief Inspector Haddock was about to make the imminent arrest of the ghost of Captain Syd, and everybody wanted to know more.

It was half day closing and Mrs Groan was holding court in the corner, repeating everything that Inspector Haddock had told her.

'Such a clever man and apparently he can do juggling too.'

'Ooh, what a talented policeman,' said one of her friends. 'I do hope Inspector Haddock makes an arrest soon. It's terrifying to think that the vengeful ghost of Captain Syd is on the loose. We might all be murdered in our beds.'

'We might,' said Mrs Groan, looking rather thrilled at the prospect. 'None of us are safe until an arrest has been made. I'm worried about all those children out in the dark at the Fancy Dress Junior Disco in the village hall when there is a murderous ghost on the loose.'

She glanced at Hetty and Tat, who had come to the table to give her and her friends more scones and jam, and said, 'I knew no good would come of all that digging for Captain Syd's lost treasure. Maybe it's you two who have brought the curse of Captain Syd down upon us all.'

Hetty glanced over to the next table where two strangers, a pair of very odd-looking and strangely hairy women, were sitting together with their heads lowered. Most people had taken no notice of them — they were far too keen to hear what Mrs Groan had to say and discuss the latest developments amongst themselves — but Hetty had been keeping a sharp eye on them. They looked so peculiar.

She suddenly remembered the bloomers

stolen from the washing line. Hetty smiled.
She was pretty certain that she knew
exactly who they were – the Ghastly
McNastys! She nudged Tat, who glanced at

the two strangers and gave Hetty a wink. Hetty knew that Tat guessed they were the McNastys too.

'Oh,' she said loudly and very casually, 'I think Tat and I can look after ourselves.'

'Yes,' said Tat. 'If those horrible, treasure-grabbing Ghastly McNastys, who are the kind of pirates who give pirates a bad name, don't frighten us, I don't think we're going to be worried by a ghost.'

Everyone groaned and snarled at the mention of the Ghastly McNastys and a few people, including Mrs Groan – who had once been the Little Snoring featherweight boxing champion – even raised their fists.

The two strange, hairy women on the next table shifted uncomfortably and if you had looked very carefully you would have seen wisps of smoke coming out of their ears. But only Hetty and Tat noticed.

'First thing tomorrow we'll be digging down at the treasure site close to the abandoned graveyard by the cliffs at the point where the beach meets the

BIG, SCARY, VERY **DARK**, DENSE FOREST

WHERE NO ONE IN THEIR RIGHT MIND WOULD WANT TO GO

AND which has got even BIGGER AND SCARIER Than it was before.

'Of course, tonight we'll be at the Little Snoring Fancy Dress Junior Disco. We are confident that tomorrow is the day that we will find Captain Syd's lost treasure. All we've got to do is dig a little further and the treasure will be ours.'

'If you don't get murdered by a ghost first,' said Mrs Groan, and she couldn't quite keep the excitement out of her voice.

'Good luck to you,' said one of her friends. 'You're braver than I am. I'm not always in my right mind but I wouldn't go to the point close to the abandoned graveyard, by the cliffs, at the point where the beach meets the

WHERE NO ONE IN THEIR RIGHT MIND WOULD WANT TO GO

not for all the treasure in the world. Not with Captain Syd's ghost in vengeful mood and already responsible for the disappearance of *The Good Hope*.'

'Me neither,' agreed everyone in the tea rooms.

Unnoticed, except by Tat and Hetty, the two strangers got up and left the tea room, their bloomers visible from under their ill-fitting skirts.

Outside, the McNastys grinned at each other, which was a horrible sight.

'Sweaty socks!' said Captain Gruesome.

'Let's go to the treasure site and dig up the treasure!'

'Squeaky pants! What a luscious idea! Let's go after dark when those horrible, revolting children will be at the Little Snoring Fancy Dress Junior Disco,' said Captain Grisly.

For once the brothers agreed.

Another Very Important Warning!
Do Not Ignore (even if you are busy juggling)!

We have had reports that not everyone has heeded the warning at the beginning of this book. It is imperative that you do not leave this book unattended at any time. The publishers have (very wisely, in my pet terrapin's humble opinion) taken the precaution of sticking the McNastys to each page using Trout's Miracle Glue.

But you can't be too careful.

DO NOT LET THIS BOOK OUT OF YOUR SIGHT. Not even when you are asleep. YOU HAVE BEEN WARNED.

The publishers cannot be held responsible
if the McNastys escape from the pages
and hold your hamster for ransom, cut off
all your sister's hair and make her cry,
steal your dad's piggy bank or eat all the
chocolate biscuits in the biscuit tin, for
which you will undoubtedly be blamed
however much you protest your innocence.

P.S. If any of you see a ferret or any fleas
or nits running around your bedroom
please stay exactly where you are and call
for help. A ferret running around your
bedroom always bodes ill, although it is
not as scary as having rioting armoured
armadillos running around your bedroom.

Chapter 7

The McNastys thought they had disposed of Jamie Fried-Trout, but just as they were wrong about so many things, they were wrong about this. All Jamie's practice holding his breath underwater in the bath had paid off. He had managed to stay under the water for infinitely longer than the McNastys thought was possible, so they had departed to Little Snoring in their rowing boat believing he was dead.

Kicking hard, Jamie shot up out of the water like a cork. Fortunately he had surfaced quite close to *The Good Hope*. Unfortunately he was not close enough to grab onto the rope ladder that hung tantalisingly close but just out of his grasp. His breath was coming in great gasps. But it wasn't going to do him much good, because he couldn't swim and, although he was only several metres from the rope ladder and safety he could just as well have been a hundred miles away in Bigbottoms-by-the-Sea.

He felt himself start sinking again. He

Jamie's cap is NOT stuck on with Trout's Miracle Glue, but fixed with excellent hair pins, as every young sailor knows.

floundered around kicking with his legs and flailing with his arms. But his panic was hindering rather than helping him. He took in a great gulp of seawater, which made him choke and splutter. He began to sink down into the water. He was going to drown. He could see his life flashing before him (which didn't take long as it had been so short) and it made him sad he would never do all the things he wanted to do, such as walk a tightrope across the Niagara Falls, win the World Tiddlywinks Championship and get first prize again for his costume at the annual Little Snoring Fancy Dress Junior Disco. His lungs hurt.

He became aware that something was nudging his bottom and pushing him upwards. The something, he realised, was a nose. A shark's nose.

So now he was not just going to drown, he was going to be eaten too! Life was so unfair!

But the shark just kept gently prodding him, and then suddenly he felt himself being wrapped in a long arm and he was raised up out of the water. He took a gulp of air. It was more delicious than strawberry ice cream.

For a moment he was held mid-air in the giant arm and then he was deposited on the deck of *The Good Hope*. He lay there gasping with shock for a few seconds and then he struggled up and peered over the side of the boat. Looking up at him were the shark (who he now recognised as the one he had helped to rid itself of the Ghastly McNastys), and the giant squid that they had so abused. The pair had saved him from drowning.

'Thank you! Thank you for saving me!' he called to them, and he bowed deeply to show his respect. The Giant Squid raised a tentacle and gave a bashful little wave.

'I'm going to thank you in the only way I can,' said Jamie. 'I'm going to find those nasty ghastly twins and make sure they are brought to justice for hijacking *The Good*

Hope and being horrible to sharks, squids and children.'

The shark put its flippers together and the squid raised two of its arms out of the water and put them together too. It was as if both creatures were clapping their approval.

Tat, Hetty, Dog, Polly and Mrs Slime
were hiding just inside the

BIG, SCARY, VERY **DARK**, DENSE FOREST

**WHERE NO ONE IN THEIR RIGHT MIND
WOULD WANT TO GO**

AND which has got
EVEN BIGGER AND SCARIER
Than it was before

in a spot from where they could keep a
good watch on the site of their treasure dig
without being seen.

108

It was not pleasant hiding there because it was not a pleasant place and it never failed to live down to its name. Already they had

had to rescue Dog from a mutant dog rose which, when he had sniffed it, had gripped his nose hard, and saved Polly from a creeping knot-weed which had tried to strangle her. Mrs Slime was none too happy either, as the children had been worried that her sneezing might alert the McNastys, so she had been obliged to wear a peg on her nose. This was extremely uncomfortable as all of you will know from those occasions (family weddings, school prize-givings) when it has been necessary to wear a peg on your nose.

Mrs Slime was beginning to feel like a human volcano that was about to explode at any moment. There was a terrible pressure building up in her nose. She just hoped her nose wouldn't fall off when she did eventually sneeze as, despite her persistent cold, she had always considered her nose – which was neither too big nor too small – one of her best features. She was worried that her face would look very odd if her nose fell off (try drawing your own

face without a nose and you will see that Mrs Slime probably had a good point).

Suddenly they all spotted a light bobbing a little way offshore and heard the splash of oars.

'This could be them,' said Tat.

Sure enough, a few minutes later, the McNastys appeared on the shore. They had changed out of the ladies' clothes and rowed round to the beach where Tat and Hetty were digging for treasure.

The children heard Gruesome tell his brother to put out his torch, but Grisly replied that there was no need. 'If they see lights it will just make those silly superstitious villagers more scared, and believe that the ghost of Captain Syd is on the rampage.'

'Smart thinking,' said Gruesome between

gritted teeth, wishing that he had thought of that.

The Ghastly McNastys crept up the beach to the place by the cliffs where the sands met the

BIG, SCARY, VERY **DARK**, DENSE FOREST

WHERE NO ONE IN THEIR RIGHT MIND
WOULD WANT TO GO

AND which has got even BIGGER

AND SCARIER

Than it was before.

They reached the big hole where Tat and Hetty had been digging for treasure and only just avoided falling into it. The hole was almost as big as a diplodocus, which is very big indeed.

The children had left two spades lying by the top of the hole because they guessed, correctly, that the McNastys would have forgotten to bring their own with them.

The McNastys grabbed the spades and climbed down the ladder into the hole and started digging greedily. They were sure that they would find the treasure very quickly.

They were so busy that they didn't notice that the children, Dog, Pegleg Polly and Mrs Slime had all left their hiding places and had very quietly made their way over to the hole.

Very stealthily, the children pulled up the ladder. The McNastys were so keen to find

the treasure
that they didn't
notice a thing.

Then Hetty got out the tube of Trout's Miracle Glue that Mr Trout had given her and squeezed it out in a thick circle all around the treasure hole. Careful to avoid stepping on the glue, they all crept back from the hole and watched with interest as the McNastys continued to dig, getting hotter and sweatier and more bad-tempered by the moment. The McNastys had taken off their shoes and socks so they could feel the cooling sand between their toes.

'Goodness, that really does look like hard work,' said Hetty very loudly, with a sweet smile.

'It does,' agreed Tat. 'I'm glad it's not us doing all that heavy spade-work. It's lovely

to have someone else to do the digging. If
they carry on they should find the treasure
for us very soon indeed. It's saved us getting
all hot and bothered. So thank you.'

The McNastys gave a squeal of fury and

rushed towards the ladder. But the ladder
was not there, and they just bumped their

heads together very hard. When they recovered, they shook their fists at the children, Mrs Slime, Dog and Polly, who all smiled back down at them very pleasantly.

'Let us out!' shouted the McNastys.

'Only if you tell us what you did with *The Good Hope* and all her crew,' said Hetty.

'Shan't!' shouted the McNastys.

The children and Mrs Slime stood up and started to stroll away.

'Wait,' shouted Captain Gruesome, thinking quickly, which sent shooting pains up and down his spine because he normally thought slower than a sloth. 'Let us out of the hole and we'll tell you.'

He winked slyly at his brother. As soon as the children and Mrs Slime put down the ladder and let them out, they would overpower them, force them down the hole and get them to do the digging for them.

'Do you promise?' asked Tat, who knew how much the McNastys' promises were worth, which was less than nothing plus nothing, which is more nothing than anyone knows what to do with.

'Of course we promise,' said the McNastys with crocodile smiles. 'We're even prepared to repent for all our ghastly nastiness in the past and promise that in the future we will give any treasure we steal . . . eh, sorry, *find* . . . to charity.'

'Do we believe them?' Tat asked Hetty with a twinkle in his eye.

'Well, they are in a bit of a hole,' said Hetty.

'Yes,' agreed Mrs Slime, 'they have dug themselves deep.'

'*Pleeeeeeeeease*,' begged the McNastys, 'we promise to be good as gold, and there's nothing gooder than gold.'

'All right, we believe you,' said Tat, but of course he didn't.

The children put down the ladder and wearily the McNastys began to climb it.

While they did, Tat scribbled a note to Inspector Haddock telling him to come to the beach and arrest the McNastys. Polly flew off with it in her beak. Then the children, Mrs Slime and Dog positioned themselves just outside the circle of glue as

the McNastys emerged from the hole.

The McNastys waited until they were both on the surface and then they launched themselves at the children. They reached out their arms and hands to grab them. Gruesome had Tat by the shoulders and Grisly had Hetty. The children pulled themselves backwards and both the McNastys toppled over from the knees. Their feet were stuck fast in Trout's Miracle Glue.

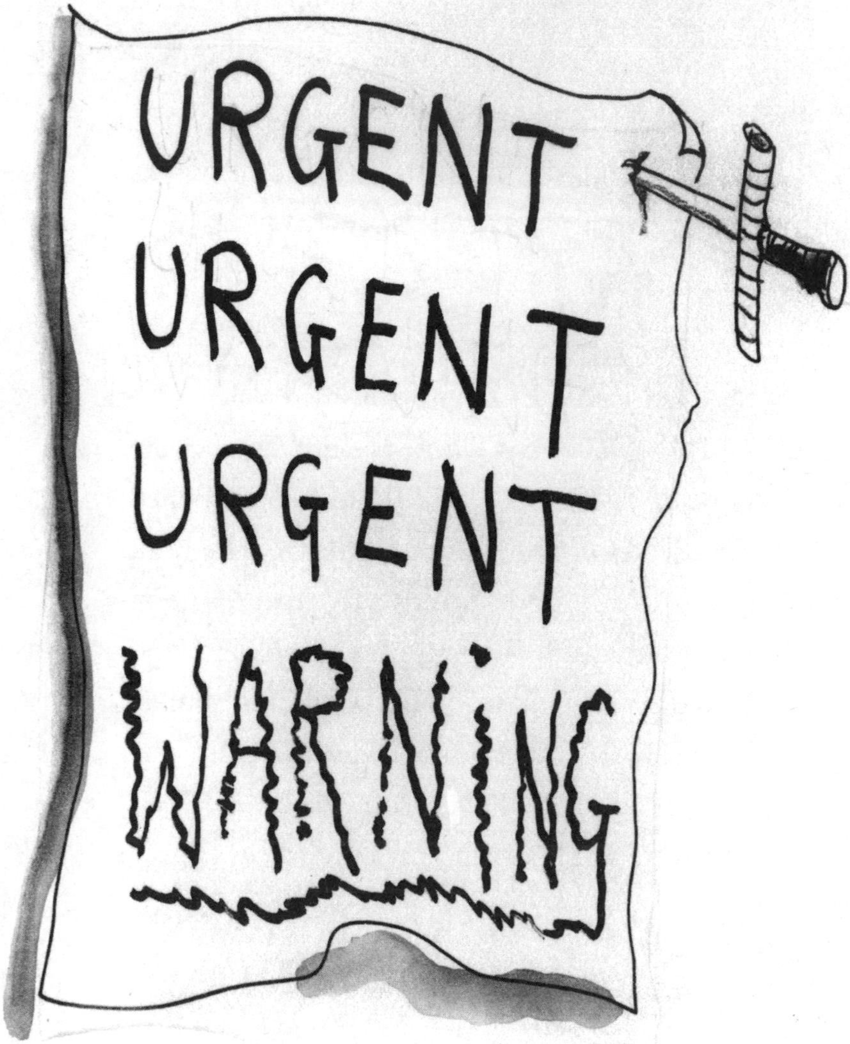
URGENT
URGENT
URGENT
WARNING

I have just received some very disturbing information. I hope you are sitting down as you may faint when you hear this frightful news. Cheapskates as ever, the publishers refused to buy Trout's Miracle Glue and instead stuck the McNastys to each page in this book using cut-price glue bought at a car boot sale at Bigbottoms-by-the-Sea.

The almost total lack of stickiness means that there is a very real danger that around page 98 the McNastys will rise from the page and rampage around your house unless you keep a sharp eye on them and only ever read this book in a locked cupboard.

Chapter 8

The McNastys gave a howl of rage as they realised what had happened. They tried to pull their feet away but they wouldn't budge. They snarled like angry armoured armadillos when they realised that they had fallen into a trap.

'Let us out!' shouted the McNastys.

'Won't,' said Tat happily, thinking that it was probably easier to get the McNastys' co-operation by telling them that he wouldn't unstick them, rather than telling them that he couldn't unstick them and that they would have to wait twenty-four hours or until Mr Trout had discovered the secret ingredient that would make Trout's Miracle Glue unstick. 'I'm afraid we will not apply the unsticking solution until you've made a full confession of everything you've done, and signed it too.'

The McNastys keep evidence of their favourite crimes in their photo album.

'Everything?' asked the McNastys, looking worried. If they confessed all the nasty ghastly things they had done they would still be confessing at Christmas, and they would also have to admit that they were the nasty killjoys behind the campaign to get Christmas and all birthdays for the under-twelves permanently cancelled.

'Just everything connected with the disappearance of *The Good Hope*, for which we are holding you responsible,' said Hetty firmly.

'Guilty as charged!' said the McNastys proudly. 'We hijacked the boat and we made all the crew walk the plank. Except that pesky little cabin boy. But we did for him, too, in the end. They're all fish food now.'

Tat felt as if somebody had removed all the bones from his legs. He sank to the ground and put his head in his hands. His cousin Jamie was dead, and all the other crew members of *The Good Hope* too. He felt terrible. They had all died because the McNastys were so greedy to get their hands on Captain Syd's lost treasure. He wished that he and Hetty had given up looking for the treasure. Maybe if they had, the Ghastly McNastys would have

given up too, and all the crew of *The Good Hope* would still be alive.

He walked away and Hetty, seeing his distress, signalled to Mrs Slime to stay and watch the McNastys, even though the McNastys were going nowhere very quickly. Their feet were quite stuck.

Hetty put her arm around Tat's shoulder and Dog put a paw in Tat's hand.

Mrs Slime kept a sharp eye on the McNastys (always better than keeping a blunt eye on someone).

'Is there really any treasure buried here?' asked Captain Gruesome. 'Or was it just a trick to get us in a hole?'

Mrs Slime took the peg off her nose because she couldn't answer with it there.

She nodded. 'Oh, the children are really confident that they are very close. Just a few more metres of digging and they will have found the treasure.' She smiled. 'And you won't even get a glimpse of it because Inspector Haddock will have arrested you and you will be locked in the Little Snoring Jail where you will only have sadness and spiders for company. The Inspector is on his way here now with his handcuffs.'

Mrs Slime felt an enormous sneeze coming on. Her nose began to tingle

dangerously. Her cold was always worse when she was stressed, and, apart from finding yourself in the middle of rioting mutant zombie armadillos, there was no greater stress in the world than finding yourself in close proximity to the McNastys. There was a noise like a thunderclap and she sneezed all over them.

AAAAATiSHOO!

The children turned. Her snot poured all over the McNastys' feet . . .

. . . and the glue immediately came unstuck!

Mrs Slime's snot was the vital missing secret ingredient for Trout's Miracle Glue (that You Can Unglue if You've Made a Terrible and Much Regretted Mistake with Your Gluing)!

But it was no moment for celebration, because immediately the McNastys threw a sack over Mrs Slime, which made her fall over. The children and Dog raced back towards the pirates. Dog got there first, but Captain Gruesome grabbed Dog and held a knife to the poor cat's throat.

'One step further, and the dratted dog – I mean mangy cat – gets it in the neck.' He grinned.

'I've always wanted to try cat burger.'

The children knew he wasn't joking. They put their hands up to show that they would offer no resistance and Captain Grisly tied Hetty and Tat and Mrs Slime's hands in front of them, tied Dog's front paws together and marched them down to the rowing boat and forced them in at knifepoint.

Then the McNastys got in themselves and started to row away from the shore.

'This is going to be fun,' said Gruesome.

'Where are you taking us?' demanded Tat.

The McNastys just grinned nastily as if they were enjoying a private joke.

'Listen!' said Hetty urgently. 'You can have the treasure if you want it so badly. Just let us go, and it's all yours. We promise.'

The McNastys cackled. They never kept any of their promises so they didn't believe anybody else's promises either.

'We're not stupid,' said Gruesome. 'We are going to dispose of you once and for all. We are going to rub you out.'

Mrs Slime began to cry quietly. She didn't want to be rubbed out – it sounded very painful.

Although Hetty felt quite like crying herself, she knew that crying was no help at all in their current dire situation.

'There is no room for melancholy in this boat,' she said kindly but firmly.

Tat glanced around the boat quickly. He hadn't realised that Melancholy Smith was with them. Then he realised his mistake – Hetty merely meant that being sad and crying wasn't going to help their situation.

The McNastys were finding rowing such a full boat very hard work, but the idea of ridding themselves of the children and their friends spurred them on.

'Where are we going?' demanded Hetty.

'You'll see soon enough,' said Gruesome happily.

It was Tat who realised first and it made his heart sink to his boots. He spied the rocks that rose from the sea like vicious teeth, which were known locally as the Jaws and that many a boat and ship had floundered on until the building of the Little Snoring lighthouse. At low tide the rocks were exposed, but at high tide they were completely submerged. The McNastys manoeuvred the boat alongside the Jaws. Then they made the children, Mrs Slime and Dog get out, and tied them all to the largest needle-like rock. 'Squeaky pants! What could be more perfect?' giggled Grisly. 'You will be able to watch us find the treasure and take it away as the water rises up over your heads!'

'Sweaty socks! We'll wave to you as we leave the beach with the treasure box,' exclaimed Gruesome happily.

Then they got back in the boat and returned to shore to claim the treasure for themselves.

The children and the others stood forlornly on the Jaws.

'Right, Hetty, any bright ideas about how we escape?' asked Tat, trying to keep his voice cheerful and not show his fear.

Hetty shook her head sadly. Everyone always said that Hetty knew everything. But she didn't have a clue how they were going to escape from the Jaws.

'A pity,' said Tat stoically, 'because the tide seems to be rising very fast indeed.'

(There was a lovely picture of Tat,
Hetty, Mrs Slime and Dog on this page
but regrettably it had been drawn in pencil
and my terrapin came along with
an eraser and they have all been
rubbed out, which is very sad
and made me cry.)

Chapter 9

Polly landed on the front desk of the police station. The desk sergeant looked at the front of the note, which was addressed to Inspector Gullible Haddock. Hetty and Tat didn't have much confidence in

Inspector Haddock's abilities to solve crimes, but he was a policeman so they were certain he would want to come to the beach and arrest the McNastys, who were always top of Little Snoring's Most Wanted list.

'I'm afraid the Inspector is busy juggling at the moment – he can't be disturbed,' the desk sergeant said.

Polly pushed the note towards the sergeant, who opened it. He could immediately see how urgent it was. The Little Snoring police force had been trying to catch the Ghastly McNastys for years.

He ran into the back room where the Inspector was trying and failing to juggle six balls.

'Sir. We've had an urgent message sent by parrot post from two children called Tat and Hetty. It says that if you go down to the beach and the place by the cliffs where the beach meets the

WHERE NO ONE IN THEIR RIGHT MIND WOULD WANT TO GO

AND which has got even **BIGGER** AND **SCARIER** Than it was before

you will be able to solve the disappearance of *The Good Hope* and arrest the Ghastly McNastys.'

'Go away!' shouted Inspector Haddock. 'I've already solved the disappearance of *The Good Hope*. The Ghastly McNastys are no longer top of Little Snoring's most wanted list. Besides, those flea- and ferret-infested varmints are miles away inside a shark. I am busy juggling and trying to work out how I'm going to arrest a ghost. I fear that dratted but undeniably clever

Hetty may have a point – it is going to be very hard to put handcuffs on a spectre. But I will use my outsize brain to solve the problem. And I will succeed. Otherwise everyone will say I'm just a big head.'

'More of a nitwit,' muttered the policeman to himself as he walked away. 'Sorry,' he said to Polly. 'That Inspector is a bit of a bird brain.' The sergeant blushed. 'My apologies, I didn't mean to be rude.'

Polly didn't mind. She knew she was smarter than Inspector Haddock and she flew away in search of Mrs Trout.

Jamie Fried-Trout was rowing across the sea towards Little Snoring. He had been so exhausted after scrambling back onto *The Good Hope* that he had fallen asleep, and by the time he woke up it was dark. The moon had come out and was shining as brightly as it could to help Jamie on his way. If Jamie was going to get revenge upon the McNastys, the moon was determined to do anything that it could to help. It didn't take kindly to being hit by dried snot pellets from the McNastys' catapults.

Jamie had changed into his costume – the ghost of Captain Syd – and planned to give Tat and Hetty an enormous surprise when he turned up at the Little Snoring Fancy Dress Junior Disco unannounced. He hoped

he might give them a bit of a fright, and of course he would be able to tell everyone that the rest of the crew from *The Good Hope* were alive and well and simply needed rescuing from the island where the shark had taken them.

He rowed hard, humming quietly to himself, when he thought he heard someone shouting 'Help!' In fact, he thought it was more than one person shouting 'Help!' Where was it coming from?

He could just see the tops of the vicious rocks known as the Jaws rising from the sea. They were almost submerged by the high tide. He knew that he should keep a safe distance from them because many a ship and boat had been wrecked on their needle-sharp teeth that were hidden underneath the water at high tide.

There was no mistaking it. Somebody was in trouble on the far side of the Jaws.

'Help!' If he wasn't mistaken, it was several people and they appeared to have a cat with them, or maybe it was a dog, it was hard to tell. There also seemed to be quite a lot of sneezing. Jamie began rowing as fast as he could around the side of the Jaws, but taking great care not to get too close.

The sea was rising fast. It was now up to the children's chests and Mrs Slime's waist. They had all frantically been trying to loosen the ropes that bound their hands together and held them fast against the rocks. But the water had made the knots tighter.

'There is no hope,' wailed Mrs Slime. Stress had made her sneeze a great deal so that the sea surrounding the Jaws had become quite snotty and the tide of goo from her nose was only adding to the rising sea level. 'We are in the jaws of death,' she wailed and nobody contradicted her because it was quite true.

'It's not over until it's over,' said Hetty firmly.

'We are rather up to our necks in it, Hetty,' said Tat.

'Actually, Tat, the water hasn't quite reached our necks,' said Hetty, who, even when she was staring death in the face, was a stickler for accuracy.

Tat said nothing as it was quite clear that

it was going to be over rather sooner than any of them would have wished. He thought he heard the sound of an oar against water. Maybe the McNastys had had a change of heart? (This doesn't mean that they had swapped hearts with somebody else but that they had suddenly become nicer and kinder, which of course is very unlikely.) Maybe Inspector Gullible Haddock had come to their rescue?

Or maybe the imminence of death was simply making him delirious so he thought he was hearing things. 'Help!' Tat shouted, but rather more faintly. There was no answering cry, but suddenly a rowing boat loomed round the side of the Jaws and headed towards them.

'Oh fishcakes,' moaned Mrs Slime between sneezes, spotting the boat and its occupant. 'We're not going to drown after all, we are going to be murdered by the vengeful ghost of Captain Syd.'

'That's not Captain Syd,' shouted Tat. 'That's my cousin, Jamie, in his fancy dress costume. I think.' He paused. 'Are you a ghost, Jamie? Did you drown and come back to haunt us in fancy dress?'

'Of course he isn't a ghost,' said Hetty.

'Hetty's right,' said Jamie, as he very

carefully lined the boat up beside the Jaws, leapt on the rocks and proceeded to untie them.

'Hetty is almost always right,' said Tat.

'I told you it wasn't over,' said Hetty, looking quite pleased with herself.

'It won't be over until we've got rid of the Ghastly McNastys,' said Jamie. 'And who knows, if we hurry, maybe we'll even get to the Little Snoring Fancy Dress Junior Disco before that's over too.'

Chapter 10

Mrs Trout was worried in the way only a mother can be, and Polly was making her more anxious flying round and round her head and clearly trying to tell her something.

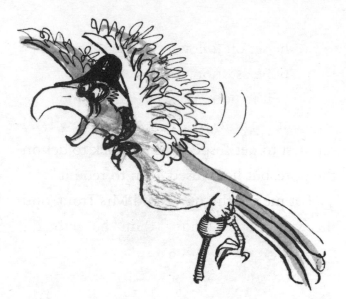

'Nasty boys, porky pies,' she kept squawking, and Mrs Trout knew that Polly was referring to the McNastys.

Mrs Trout had every faith in Tat and Hetty and knew that they were more than a match for the McNastys but she had been expecting them home to change into their fancy dress costumes and they hadn't turned up.

So she set off following Polly who led her to the police station.

'Oh, it's you back again,' said the sergeant when he saw Polly. 'You know I did my best to get Inspector Haddock to act on the note, but he refused even to read it.'

'Let me see the note,' said Mrs Trout, and she sounded so angry that the sergeant handed it over without a squeak.

'Good girl, Polly,' said Mrs Trout when she had read it, and she pushed the desk sergeant aside and strode into the back room.

'You can't go in there . . .' he began.

But she had. She found Inspector Gullible Haddock standing in the middle of the room trying to hula-hoop very badly.

Mrs Trout was furious.

It wasn't the Inspector's dismal

incompetence at the hula-hoop that made Mrs Trout so angry (although he clearly had absolutely no talent for it at all and was wasting his and the hula-hoop's time) but the fact that Tat, Hetty, Dog and Mrs Slime were facing the Ghastly McNastys all alone.

She was as angry as a lioness who realises that her cubs are being threatened. She marched right up to Inspector Haddock who dropped his hula-hoop in surprise.

'Why did you ignore the message from Tat and Hetty about the Ghastly McNastys being down on the beach?' she demanded.

Inspector Haddock gave a snooty smile. 'I ignored it because I have already solved the case of *The Good Hope*. In this instance the Ghastly McNastys are innocent.'

'The Ghastly McNastys are never innocent,' roared Mrs Trout, 'and I've heard your theory about the ghost of Captain Syd being responsible for the disappearance of *The Good Hope* and it's complete codswallop. At this very moment two children, a cat, and a lady with a very persistent cold who should be tucked up warm in bed with a hot water bottle, are facing up to the McNastys all on their own while you fiddle around learning circus skills and trying to dream up ways to arrest a ghost that doesn't even exist.'

She put her face very close to Inspector Haddock's face. 'Do you know what you are?'

'The world's greatest detective?' mumbled Inspector Haddock more in hope than expectation.

'You are a complete clown!' said Mrs Trout and all the rest of the Little Snoring police force, who had been listening just outside the door, broke into loud laughter. 'And you are coming with me to find out what's happened to those brave children, and arrest the Ghastly McNastys.' She turned to the rest of the Little Snoring police force. 'And you'd better all come too. Things may get very nasty and ghastly.'

At the same time as Mrs Trout arrived at the police station, the children, Dog and Mrs Slime arrived at the Trout family home. Tat and Hetty changed into their skeleton costumes.

They added a few pirate touches such as eye-patches and hats. They even found skeleton costumes for Mrs Slime and Dog.

Then they took full pots of luminous paint and all the remaining supplies of Trout's Miracle Glue from the garden shed and hurried down the path towards the beach where they had left the rowing boat.

With Tat and Jamie rowing as hard and fast as they could, they soon arrived at the secluded cove where *The Good Hope* was moored. Mrs Slime and Jamie quickly set to work hoisting the mast back in place and securing it with Trout's Miracle Glue. 'Just make sure you don't sneeze over it,' Tat told Mrs Slime.

Meanwhile the others set about painting the ship all over with luminous paint. Very conveniently, at that moment Polly, who had been flying around the island looking for them, arrived and proved a dab beak with her paintbrush. She flew around the outside of the ship in record time and daubed it in a thick layer of paint.

'Now all we need is for the moon to shine very brightly so the paint gets really luminous and then disappears behind a cloud at exactly the right moment,' said Hetty. 'Goodness,' she said looking up in the sky, which had suddenly become enormously bright, 'it's almost as if the moon heard me.' She gave a little laugh. 'But of course that's impossible. It would be like believing in ghosts.'

At the treasure site, the McNastys were feeling more than a little spooked. They knew that they, not the ghost of Captain Syd, were responsible for the disappearance of *The Good Hope*, but that didn't stop them worrying that he might take his revenge on them when they found the treasure. They

jumped at the smallest sound. At one point an owl had hooted and they had both tried to jump into the other's arms and instead had ended up on the ground.

They were also uncomfortably hot again. They had been digging for ages and there was still no sign of the treasure. They were beginning to think that they had been tricked again, and they would have rowed back out to the Jaws to punch the children very hard if it was not for the fact that it would be too much like hard work to climb up the ladder. They were also eager to find the treasure quickly so that Tat, Hetty and the others would see them with the treasure chest before the water covered their faces and they drowned. As they were down in the hole digging, they hadn't seen the children being rescued by Jamie.

The McNastys were rather regretting that they hadn't got the children and Mrs Slime to do the digging for them and then

buried them alive in the hole once they had found the treasure. Each of the McNastys blamed the other for not thinking of that.

'What we need is a helping hand,' said Gruesome.

'Nobody ever wants to help us,' said Grisly mournfully.

'Maybe we can entice some children away from the Junior Disco and force them to dig for us,' mused Gruesome.

Suddenly Grisly smiled a cunning smile.

'I've got a much better idea. I've got an idea that will go with a bang.' And he climbed up the ladder, ran down to the rowing boat and found the six sticks of dynamite, some fuse wire and a box of

matches that he had brought from the ship. He was so excited that he didn't notice the children were no longer tied to the Jaws. 'We'll blast our way to the treasure!'

Gruesome sniffed. He didn't want to show his brother that he was impressed by his smart thinking, but he thought it was the best idea that Grisly had ever had. Even better than the time that he had stolen all the ice creams from the children on the beach at Bigbottoms-by-the-Sea.

More evidence
of the McNastys' crimes

Very quickly, the pirates laid the dynamite and then they ran a fuse until they judged that they were far enough away to be quite safe.

They were just about to light it when they heard shouting from the top of the beach.

Racing towards them was the entire Little Snoring police force, led by Inspector Haddock. The police all had their handcuffs at the ready. Following them was Mrs Trout who was waving her umbrella, and quite honestly she was the scariest sight of all. Even more scary than a rioting armoured armadillo or the vengeful ghost of Captain Syd.

She was yelling, 'What have you done with my Tat and Hetty? I'll have your guts for garters if you've touched a hair on their heads.'

I'll have your guts for garters!

The McNastys looked at each other. They knew they ought to run, but the lure of the treasure was too great. They nodded at each other and then they both struck a match and lit the fuse. A river of sparks ran along the fuse and down into the hole.

Inspector Gullible Haddock had just

seized both McNastys by the scruff of the
neck, utterly thrilled to be arresting them
finally, when there was an enormous
explosion. The whole beach seemed to
shudder as if it had been hit by a massive
earthquake, and everyone was swept off
their feet.

There was a terrible silence on the beach. The McNastys were the first to recover. They rushed to the edge of the hole and peered into it. They spied

The McNastys were so thrilled that they screamed with delight, a noise so horrible it was like the sound of forty jet airplanes landing just outside your bedroom window.

They stretched out their arms towards the treasure – and at that very moment there was another sound as if the earth itself was cracking in two, and the cliffs by the treasure site developed hundreds of fissures and fractures as a result of the McNastys' screams.

There was a moment when it seemed as if time stood still. And then, as if in slow motion, the front part of the cliffs tumbled downwards towards the treasure site. The McNastys only just jumped out of the way before thousands of tons of rock fell into the hole and covered it over completely. For a second everyone stood there completely stunned.

Then the McNastys burst into tears and

began scrabbling at the huge rocks with their hands.

But it was useless. The treasure was buried, almost certainly for ever.

The smoke and debris began to clear and when the McNastys, no longer blinded by the dazzle of the treasure, looked at what remained of the cliff they saw a truly terrible and fearsome sight – a huge and ferocious skeleton monster was looming over them.

In their confusion and dazed state, the McNastys decided that it must be a ghost monster come to get them.

They gave a scream of fright and began to run towards their rowing boat at the edge of the sea.

But just as they reached it, they saw a huge ghostly pirate ship coming towards them. The entire ship was emitting an eerie green, including the skull and crossbones that Jamie had taken from his pocket and which now flew from the top of the (slightly wonky) mast.

And worst of all, as far as the Ghastly McNastys were concerned, leering at them from the prow of the ship and shaking his cutlass at them was what was unmistakeably the ghost of Captain Syd.

It was ten times more frightening than anything they had ever seen before, and it was accompanied by a host of pirate skeletons that were all pointing their bony fingers at the McNastys, like fingers of judgement.

'I'm coming to get you, boys,' roared Captain Syd, and the ship ploughed its way towards them and appeared to be about to run straight onto the beach and the place where they were standing.

The McNastys whimpered and shrieked. They didn't know which way to turn. They were caught between the ghost monster on the cliffs and the spectre of Captain Syd and his eerie glowing pirate ship in the water, and the Little Snoring police force and Mrs Trout who were bearing down on them from the left.

The McNastys decided to run to the right. They ran along the beach as fast and as far away from the ship as they could and they then plunged into the sea, completely forgetting that neither of them could really swim very well.

They took several strokes and were carried by the retreating tide further out to sea. They tried to take another stroke and instead swallowed great gulps of water. They spluttered and were about to sink, when a huge tentacle emerged from the ocean and curled around them both. They screamed and they shrieked as the giant squid swum off holding them aloft. Their shrieks and screams grew fainter and fainter.

As soon as they disappeared over the horizon, Tat, Hetty, Jamie and the others put down the anchor, climbed down the side of the ship, got into the rowing boat and came ashore.

'Calm down, Mum, we're quite safe,' said Tat happily as Mrs Trout hugged him, Jamie and Hetty.

The children and Mrs Slime explained to Mrs Trout and Inspector Haddock everything that had happened and how the McNastys had admitted that they had been responsible for the disappearance of *The Good Hope*. Jamie also explained to the coastguard, who had been summoned by the police, where the island was where the crew of *The Good Hope* were stranded. A boat was sent to rescue them immediately.

'Well,' said Mrs Trout, 'I'm sorry that after all your hard work, Captain Syd's treasure is buried and probably lost for ever. But it's been more trouble than it's worth, and I'm just pleased that you are all safe and sound. It's a pity that Inspector Haddock didn't get to arrest the Ghastly McNastys so we were rid of them once and for all.'

'He can always arrest me as the ghost of Captain Syd!' piped up Jamie with a wicked smile.

Inspector Haddock turned scarlet and crept away feeling completely humiliated. He vowed to give up being a detective; he felt that maybe clowning was his true vocation.

'Of course,' said Hetty, 'we may not have uncovered the treasure but we have discovered something very valuable.' She pointed at the cliff. 'I'm pretty sure that is the first time that the complete skeleton of a diplodocus has been discovered. I rather think that the dinosaur professors are going to be very interested.'

'Oi, Dog! Put that bone down,' shouted Tat, seeing Dog attempt to put an eight-metre diplodocus bone in his mouth. 'You can't eat that. It's 150 million years old. It will be mouldier than most of the food in Mrs Groan's shop. We'll get you a nice fresh bone from the butchers.'

Dog obediently did as he was told and bounded over to lick Tat's face.

Chapter 11

Tat, Hetty and Jamie left the village hall and sat outside on the steps overlooking the sea, eating their bowls of ice cream. The Little Snoring Fancy Dress Junior Disco was still in full swing. Even though they had arrived late, it had been a lovely evening. Jamie had once again won first prize for his 'ghost of Captain Syd' costume in the fancy dress competition.

Mr Trout had been delighted to hear that Mrs Slime's snot was the secret ingredient for Trout's Miracle Glue, and was convinced that his invention would have a bright commercial future. It had already come in handy half an hour earlier when Melancholy Smith's elder sister stuck her to the village hall toilet seat after Melancholy beat her in the fancy dress competition.

'See,' said Mr Trout, 'it's always happening. There will be a massive demand for Trout's Miracle Glue.'

The coastguard had turned up with the crew of *The Good Hope* just as the sausages and baked potatoes were being served, which was lucky as they were very hungry as they had been living on berries and coconuts for the last few days. The captain had been delighted to hear that her boat was intact thanks to Jamie and the others, even if it was covered in luminous green paint and the mast was a bit wobbly. The last few days had seemed like a nightmare that was all over now.

There had also been a call from Greater Snoring University.

The world-famous dinosaur expert, Professor Dino Fossil, would be at the cliffs at first light and was very excited about the find.

The children finished their ice cream and wandered onto the beach. It was a brilliantly bright moonlit night, as if the moon had decided it had something to celebrate.

'Tat,' asked Jamie, 'do you mind that Captain Syd's lost treasure is probably buried for ever under that rock fall?'

Tat shook his head. 'Not really. A diplodocus is much more exciting.'

'At least the McNastys are out of our hair,' said Hetty (who didn't mean that the McNastys had been living on her and Tat's heads but that they had been a great nuisance). 'From what you tell us, Jamie, I reckon that giant squid means business.'

Jamie nodded.

'Yes,' said Tat, 'maybe we shouldn't press our luck and we should give up treasure hunting.'

'It's not over until it's over,' said a quiet voice behind them.

The children spun round. An elderly pirate was standing there. He wasn't threatening or vengeful at all and he had a twinkle in his eye and he looked very, very familiar, from pictures they had all seen in books.

'Captain Syd . . .?' asked Tat with wonder in his voice.

The pirate smiled and tipped his hat at them and winked, and as he did so he began to disappear.

Eventually all that was left of him was his smile hanging in the air and then that also vanished.

'Hetty,' said Tat firmly, 'I know you don't

182

believe in them, but I've definitely maybe just seen a ghost.'

'Me too,' said Hetty. 'Definitely. Maybe.'

JAN 2017

come aboard,
me hearties!

ghastlymcnastys.co.uk

Go online for
pirate puzzles,
dastardly downloads,
ghastly games
and more!